W9-APS-579

HASBRO and its logo, MY LITTLE PONY and all related characters are trademarks of Hasbro and are used with permission. © 2017 Hasbro. All Rights Reserved.

Cover design by Carolyn Bull.

Hachette Book Group supports the right to free expression and the value of copyright. The purpose of copyright is to encourage writers and artists to produce the creative works that enrich our culture.

The scanning, uploading, and distribution of this book without permission is a theft of the author's intellectual property. If you would like permission to use material from the book (other than for review purposes), please contact permissions@hbgusa.com. Thank you for your support of the author's rights.

Little, Brown and Company
Hachette Book Group
1290 Avenue of the Americas, New York, NY 10104
Visit us at lb-kids.com
mylittlepony.com

First Edition: May 2017

LB kids is an imprint of Little, Brown and Company.
The LB kids name and logo are trademarks of Hachette Book Group, Inc.

The publisher is not responsible for websites (or their content) that are not owned by the publisher.

Library of Congress Control Number 2016958930

ISBNs: 978-0-316-43176-7 (paperback); 978-0-316-55367-4 (ebook); 978-0-316-55398-8 (ebook); 978-0-316-43177-4 (ebook)

Printed in the United States of America.

CW

10 9 8 7 6 5 4 3 2 1

Licensed By:

Rainbow Dash and the Great Cookie Prank

Adapted by Magnolia Belle

Based on the episode

"28 Pranks Later" written by F. M. De Marco

LITTLE, BROWN & COMPANY

LB kids

It's a dark and spooky night, and Fluttershy is trotting home through the woods with some of her animal pals. She hears something lurking in the darkness and starts to run.

The scary noises get louder and a creature jumps out from behind some bushes. Fluttershy screams and shuts her eyes. She hears laughter and opens them again. The frightening creature is just Rainbow Dash playing a prank.

The next morning, Fluttershy calls a meeting at Twilight's Castle of Friendship to talk about Rainbow Dash's pranks and how they are getting out of hoof. Pinkie Pie thinks the pranks are hilarious, but the other ponies don't all agree. Rainbow Dash vows to double her pranking efforts and storms out of the meeting.

Later, at Rarity's Carousel Boutique, Rarity is trying to sew a new Filly Guide uniform for Sweetie Belle when her sewing machine falls apart. The machine is just made of cake!

"Your sewing machine is yummy!" Sweetie Belle says, as she eats a big piece of sewing machine.

Rainbow Dash jumps out and laughs. "Gotcha!" she shouts.

Applejack wants to make sure she has a good night's sleep free of Rainbow Dash's sneaky pranks. She sets up alarms and traps all around her bed and goes to sleep. In the morning, she wakes up to find her bed is in the pigpen! "Gotcha!" Rainbow Dash yells.

Rainbow Dash pranks everypony in Ponyville—
from Cranky Doodle Donkey to Big McIntosh—
laughing and yelling "Gotcha!" each time.

Rainbow Dash's friends go to Pinkie Pie to ask for help in dealing with all the pranking.

Twilight Sparkle makes a plea to Pinkie Pie. "Pranks are not for everypony. It doesn't seem like Rainbow Dash is taking the time to find out who enjoys them and who doesn't."

"Yeah, we thought you might be able to get her to cut it out," Applejack says.

Later, Pinkie Pie tries to tell Rainbow Dash that she should not prank as much because it's upsetting the other ponies.

Before Pinkie Pie can say anything, Rainbow Dash gives her a cookie. Pinkie Pie gobbles up the cookie, and Rainbow Dash giggles.

"What's so funny?" Pinkie asks.

Rainbow Dash tells Pinkie Pie that it's a joke cookie. She special ordered them, and anypony who eats them will get a big surprise: They turn ponies' mouths different colors!

Rainbow Dash brags, "I'm gonna switch them with the Filly Guide cookies that Scootaloo and her friends are selling. Everypony in town is gonna get a rainbow-colored mouth, courtesy of *Rainbow* Dash! It's gonna be *so* awesome!"

Pinkie Pie is nervous about Rainbow Dash's plan. "Maybe this is a good time to stop pranking for a *little* while," she says.

Rainbow Dash roars, "*Stop*?! No! Way! This prank is happening, Pinkie, and it's gonna be *hilarious*!" She has never been prouder.

Rainbow Dash tells Pinkie to meet in the morning so she can help her switch out all the Filly Guide cookies for joke cookies.

But in the morning, Pinkie Pie doesn't show up to help Rainbow Dash pull off her big prank. Rainbow Dash gets angry and storms into Pinkie Pie's room to ask why she didn't help. Rainbow Dash is shocked to find Pinkie Pie is sick in bed!

Pinkie Pie coughs. "I haven't been feeling well. The only thing that makes me feel any better is these cookies. You don't have any more, do you?"

Rainbow Dash replies, "No, I told you, I used all the cookies for the prank. Pretty soon everypony in town will have a rainbow-color mouth and they'll know it was me who pranked them so well! Come on, Pinkie. You don't want to miss it!"

Pinkie Pie tells Rainbow Dash that she is much too sick to go and probably can't even stand up. "Unless you've got more **cookies?!**" She begs Rainbow Dash for more cookies.

Rainbow Dash is a little freaked out and suggests that Pinkie Pie stay home and rest.

The Cutie Mark Crusaders gather at Sweet Apple Acres to get ready to go out and sell their Filly Guide cookies all over Ponyville. Rainbow Dash is there to make sure her prank goes off without a hitch, but she *tells* them she's really just there to help.

Applejack doesn't trust Rainbow Dash to not pull any pranks and says she'll keep a close eye on her.

"Let's go!" Scootaloo commands. "We've got a lot of ground to cover if we wanna hit every house in Ponyville!"

"Come on, you heard her! Every house in Ponyville. Heh, heh, heh." Rainbow Dash laughs as she takes tremendous pride in her brilliant plan.

The Cutie Mark Crusaders and their chaperones make visits to every house in Ponyville. They sell cookies to Fluttershy. They sell cookies to Princess Twilight Sparkle and Spike. Even Big McIntosh, Miss Cheerilee, Cranky Doodle Donkey, and the Cake family all buy cookies.

Rainbow Dash cannot contain her giddy laughter. She laughs and laughs and laughs after every cookie sale. The other ponies don't seem to notice or mind her laughter.

Applejack and Rarity praise the Cutie Mark
Crusaders for such a hard day's work.
   "Y'all should be real proud of yourselves today.
Don't you think so, Rainbow Dash?"

Rainbow Dash isn't paying attention. She is too focused on the town and waiting for ponies to burst out of their homes with rainbow mouths.

"Any minute now..." Rainbow Dash mutters to herself as she twirls her hooves.

Applejack says, "Uh, 'any minute now' what?"

"Hm? Oh! Nothing. Don't you guys think the town is a little too quiet?" Rainbow Dash asks nervously.

Rarity responds, "Of course it's quiet. Ponies can't talk while they're eating those fabulous cookies! They are probably all in a cookie coma by now!"

Rainbow Dash is worried she might miss her prank's payoff.

Rainbow Dash bolts off to check on everypony who bought cookies.

She peers into window after window, but there is no pony to be found. Just empty cookie boxes.

"What is going on?" she asks herself. "Everypony should be running through the streets with rainbow mouths!"

Pinkie Pie is the only pony who knows Rainbow Dash's secret prank, so Rainbow goes to see her for support.

The lights are all out at Sugarcube Corner. Rainbow Dash assumes Pinkie is still sick in bed. She stumbles through the dark and starts to worry that there might be something wrong with her joke cookies.

Rainbow Dash hears some pots clanging in the kitchen. She spies Mrs. Cake in the darkness and lets out a sigh of relief.

"Mrs. Cake! *Phew.* Have you seen Pinkie?" Rainbow Dash asks, but Mrs. Cake doesn't respond. "Uh. Mrs. Cake?"

Mrs. Cake steps out of the darkness and the moonlight reveals her face is covered in rainbow colors. **"Cookies!!!"** she utters with a deep rasp.

Rainbow Dash panics and stumbles backward. She falls to the ground. Before she can get back up and run away, Pinkie Pie busts out of a cupboard and belts out a blood-curdling groan. **"Coooookiesss!"**

Rainbow Dash screams in terror and flies away as fast as she can.

Out on the street, Rainbow Dash is confronted by
more cookie craving ponies.

"Cookies!!" they utter as they stagger toward her.
She takes off in the opposite direction.

Rainbow Dash spots Twilight Sparkle and Spike from far away and flies toward them for help.

She shouts, "Twilight! You gotta help. Something's going on in Ponyville! Ponies are turning into cookie zombies!"

Twilight Sparkle doesn't respond. Rainbow Dash approaches slowly. As she gets closer, Twilight and Spike turn and reveal faces covered in rainbow colors. **"Coooookiess!"** they both rasp.

Rainbow Dash tries to get help from other ponies.
She goes to see Fluttershy and the Apple Family, but
they are all cookie zombies, too!

Rainbow Dash flies back to Applejack, Rarity, and the Cutie Mark Crusaders and is relieved to find that they are still normal.

"Don't eat any cookies!" she shouts at them.

They look at her like she is crazy. Then they see something even crazier behind Rainbow Dash. It's a horde of cookie-zombie ponies coming right at them!

The healthy ponies barricade themselves in a barn.

Sweetie Belle looks out the window and cries, "What happened to all of our friends?"

Rainbow Dash confesses that she switched the regular cookies with joke cookies and now everypony who eats them turns into a cookie-craving zombie.

The cookie zombies outside start to break into the barn. Even Applejack, Rarity, and the Cutie Mark Crusaders are cookie-crazy now!

Rainbow Dash cowers in the corner. She pleads, "This was just a harmless prank! It was supposed to be funny, *but this is NOT funny*!"

"Exactly!" Pinkie Pie laughs.

Rainbow Dash uncovers her eyes. She's confused. "What?" she asks.

Applejack says, "How does it feel to get a taste of your own medicine?"

The ponies reveal that they were just pranking back Rainbow Dash to teach her a lesson: Not everypony enjoys pranks.

They all shout, "*Gotcha!*"